HEY, Rabbit!

SERGIO RUZZIER

A Neal Porter Book
Roaring Brook Press
New York

To Karen.

Thanks to Viola for her precious help.

A Neal Porter Book
Published by Roaring Brook Press
Roaring Brook Press is a division of Holtzbrinck Publishing Holdings Limited Partnership
175 Fifth Avenue, New York, New York 10010
www.roaringbrookpress.com

Distributed in Canada by H. B. Fenn and Company Ltd.

Cataloging-in-Publication Data is on file at the Library of Congress
ISBN: 978-1-59643-502-5

Roaring Brook Press books are available for special promotions and premiums.
For details contact: Director of Special Markets, Holtzbrinck Publishers.

First Edition February 2010
Book design by Barbara Grzeslo
Printed in December 2009 in China by Toppan Leefung Printing Ltd.,
    Dongguan City, Guangdong Province

10 9 8 7 6 5 4 3 2

"HEY, Rabbit! Is there anything for me in your suitcase? Maybe a bone for my birthday?"

"HEY, Rabbit! Is there anything for me in your suitcase? Maybe a leaf to remind me of home?"

"HEY, Rabbit! Is there anything for me in your suitcase? Maybe a pillow for my sleepy head?"

"HEY, Rabbit! Is there anything for me in your suitcase? Maybe a ball of twine to play with?"

"HEY, Rabbit! Is there anything for me in your suitcase? Maybe a piece of cheese for my empty belly?"

"HEY, Rabbit! Is there anything for me in your suitcase? Maybe a shell with the sound of the sea?"

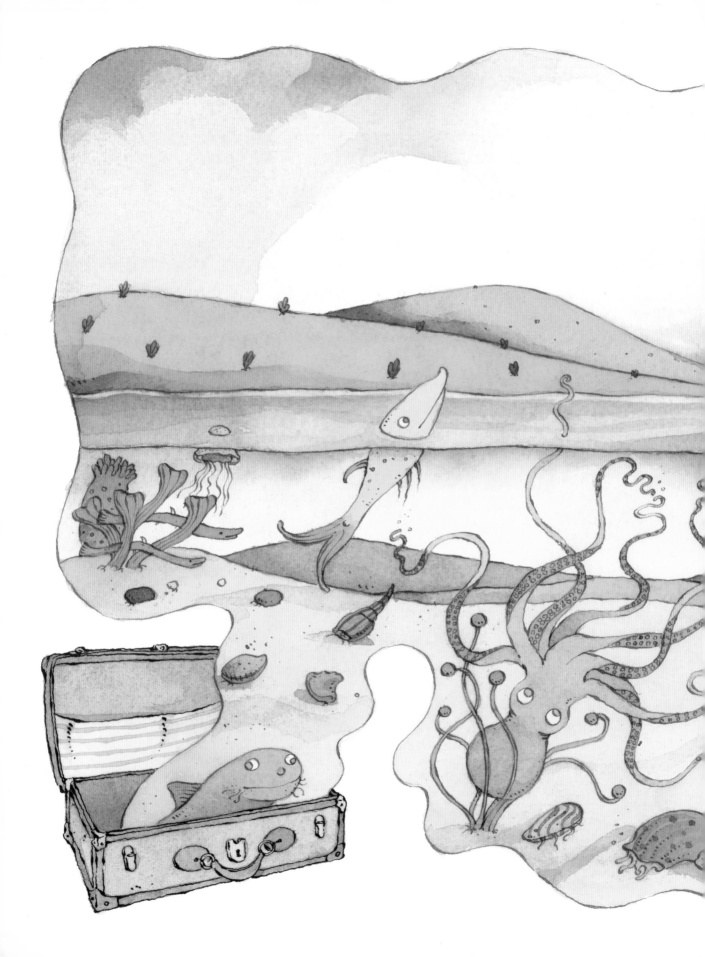

"HEY …Is there anything for *me* in my suitcase?"